What I Do Know

By Lori Schlecht

Illustrated by D.C. Ice

For my boys, JP and Eli
—Lori

ISBN 13: 978-1-59298-688-0

Library of Congress Catalog Number: 2015919353

Printed in the United States of America

First Printing: 2016

20 19 18 17 16   5 4 3 2 1

Cover and interior design by Laura Drew.
Illustrated by D.C. Ice
Edited by Lily Coyle.

Beaver's Pond Press
7108 Ohms Lane
Edina, MN 55439–2129
952-829-8818
www.beaverspondpress.com

BEAVER'S POND
PRESS

My Dear, Precious Child,

When I watch you sleeping, or running around giggling,
or especially when we celebrate your birthday,
I long to know more about you. I have a longing—
a longing to give you the answers you deserve,
to tell you the stories that all parents tell.
There's so much I don't know about you,
and so much I wish I could say.

When I ponder all that I do not know,
I remember how blessed we are,
and what a joy it is to tell you
what I do know.

I don't know about the day you were born.

But I do know that the day I saw your sweet face
and held you in my arms, we belonged to each other.

I don't know if anyone was there to welcome
you on the day of your birth.

But I do know you were welcomed home by your new forever family and friends with signs, gifts, balloons, and so much unconditional love.

I don't know what your first word was.

But I do know how it warmed my heart when you first sweetly said, "I love you."

I don't know what your first food was.

But I do know that as we gather around our kitchen table each night,
you'll always have food and family togetherness to be thankful for.

I don't know a lot about your heritage.

But I do know that I'll always honor who you are.

We'll learn and research and celebrate that beautiful piece of you, together.

I don't know where you were
when you smiled for the first time.

But I do know that whenever you smile, you light up the entire room you're in.

I don't know a lot of information about your birth family.

But I do know that you're part of the heart and soul of our family.

We would not be complete without you.

I'm the luckiest person in the world because I get to be your parent.

I don't know what your first toy was.

But I do know that your life will be filled with toys, activities, and relationships that inspire you to be creative, to be silly, and to grow.

I don't know where you were
when you let out your first coo or giggle.

But I do know that we will share much joy and laughter
as we journey through life together.

I don't know where you were
when you cried your first tear.

But I do know that for the rest of my life,
I'll be there to comfort you and wipe your tears away.

I don't know what memories you hold
or what questions you will ask me in the future.

But I do know I'll be by your side, loving and supporting you
as we take this amazing journey through life together.